TABLE OF CONTENTS

DID YOU KNOW?

Winifred sold **30,000** records a week at the height of her fame. She has now been commemorated with a black plaque in South London.

WHO WAS ...

WINIFRED ATWELL?

1914-1983

Winifred was the first Black person to have a number one hit in the UK Singles Chart.

1 Una Winifred Atwell was a pianist born on 27th February 1914, in Trinidad.

2 Winifred was popular in Britain and Australia in the 1950s with a series of boogie-woogie and ragtime hits, selling over 20 million records.

3 She had studied the piano as a child and by the age of 30 wanted to be trained in the USA.

4 By the mid 1940s she had gained a place at London's Royal Academy of Music and she wanted to become a concert pianist. To finance this initiative, she had to work during the evenings at clubs in London playing piano rags. By 1950, her popularity had begun to spread nationally. She began recording her music in around 1951.

5 Winifred's music also worked well on TV where she made regular appearances. She would usually start her act by playing a classical piece on a grand piano before moving to what she called "my other piano" which was an old "honky tonk" upright. It was on this that she recorded many of her most successful numbers. In total, she had 11 UK top ten hits including 'Britannia Rag', 'Let's Have A Party', 'Let's Have Another Party' and 'The Poor People Of Paris'. She recorded 'Black And White Rag' in 1952 and it later became the theme tune for the BBC's *Pot Black* snooker programme for several decades.

ALANA-MAE

DENZEL

MALAYÀ

I AM CROWNED IN MY *curls*

"My hair is the perfect halo for my head. It's stunning, strong and soft all at the same time."

AIDEN

JADYN

MYA-RAE

Hello

"Take a look at our beautiful gallery of Cocoa Kids who love and embrace their hair."

SLAY

ZARA

"MY HAIR IS BEAUTIFUL! I AM A QUEEN CROWNED IN CURLS"

I ♥ ME

NAHLA-MAI

"I love my hair because it is full, thick, natural and curly. The best thing about my hair is that when it is washed it goes really short, then Mummy makes it long again. My hair is magic."

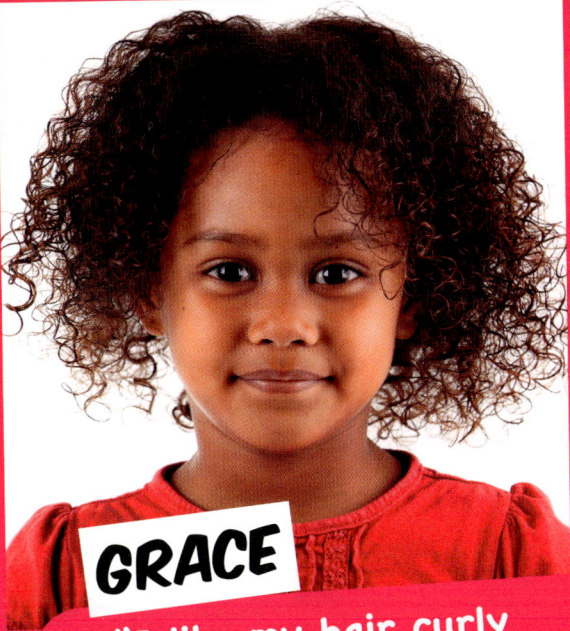

GRACE

"I like my hair curly and sometimes I wear it straight. I love the compliments on how lovely my hair is."

ANDRE

KING

TAI

LEO

NOAH

"My mummy is amazing and styles my hair in lots of different ways."

SIENNA

DESIGN YOUR OWN HOODIE

Colour in the hoodie below and create a logo to make your own design.

NATURAL Beauty

BY NILE

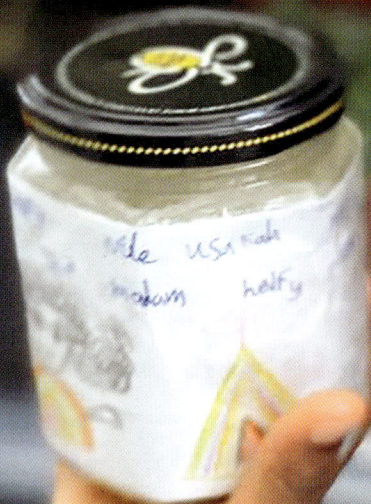

"I really admire Madam C.J. Walker. She made her own haircare products and became a millionaire."

> "Hi! My name is Nile and I am the beauty editor in this issue of Cocoa magazine.
>
> Today I am going to share the ingredients for my healthy home-made hair cream that I made with my mummy."

Nile's Healthy Hair Cream Ingredients

- 1/2 cup of unrefined white or yellow shea butter
- 1/4 cup of aloe vera gel
- 2 tablespoons of organic coconut oil

"My hair feels really great after using my home-made hair cream. We mixed the ingredients together with a kitchen mixer and the hair cream was nice and fluffy. This can be used as body butter too."

NEVER TRY THIS ON YOUR OWN
Adult supervision is required when making this hair cream.

You could draw something like this.

WHY NOT MAKE YOUR OWN COCONUT OIL MOISTURISER!

NEVER TRY THIS ON YOUR OWN

INGREDIENTS

1. 1 cup of coconut oil
2. 1/2 teaspoon of vitamin E oil
3. 1-3 drops of lavender oil

Mix all ingredients together and store in a cool place.

1

2

3

Many skin and hair products include harsh chemicals. If you have dry and sensitive skin, natural recipes such as this can help to hydrate and soothe any irritation.

cocoa

Make a label like the one above to stick on your home-made moisturiser.

Eczema is the name for a group of skin conditions that cause dry, irritated skin.
Types of eczema include:

● discoid eczema – a type of eczema that occurs in circular or oval patches on the skin

● contact dermatitis – a type of eczema that occurs when the body comes into contact with a particular substance

Yeah!

RAHEEM STERLING

Raheem Shaquille Sterling (born 8th December 1994) is an English professional footballer who plays as a winger for Premier League club Chelsea and the England national team.

Born in Jamaica to Jamaican parents, Raheem moved to London at the age of 5 and began his career at Queens Park Rangers before signing to Liverpool in 2010. He was awarded the Golden Boy award in 2014. He also won the PFA Young Player of the Year and FWA Footballer of the Year.

I am loving

I am loyal

I am polite

Repeat these positive affirmations to yourself every morning in the mirror. Affirmations are positive motivational messages. When you repeat them often, and believe in them too, you can start to make positive changes.

I am clever

I am faithful

I am kind

I am optimistic

I am intelligent

16

Voyage to *Africa*

LET'S VISIT ...

NIGERIA

Home to over **211 million** people in 2021, Nigeria has the sixth largest population in the whole world and is often called the 'Giant of Africa'. Its official name is the Federal Republic of Nigeria. Most of the country is made up of young people, and around 40% of the entire population are under the age of 14 — that's a lot of future leaders!

What is the population of Nigeria?

NATURE

Nigeria is located in Western Africa with four other African countries around its borders. The Niger River flows from Niger (to the north) and through Nigeria. The Niger River is where both countries get their similar names from.

The Gulf of Guinea is part of the Atlantic and runs all the way along Nigeria's southern borders, with Chad and Cameroon to the east. Benin, believed to be the original home of the great 'Benin Bronzes', is situated to the west.

NIGERIA

FUN FACTs

NIGERIA

OFFICIAL NAME Federal Republic of Nigeria

CAPITAL Abuja

POPULATION 211 million people

COUNTRY SIZE 923,768 square kilometres

LANGUAGE English

MONEY Naira

Lagos is one of the most urban and modern cities and was once Nigeria's capital — many people still believe it is. In 1991, Abuja was renamed the capital city by federal decree and still remains the capital today.

Nigeria is often called the 'Giant of Africa'. This name comes from the vastness of its land, the diversity of its peoples and languages, its huge population (the largest in Africa), and its oil and other natural resources.

PEOPLE AND CULTURE

School is different for our Nigerian brothers and sisters. Most children start primary school at the age of 5 and study for six years before they can move on to secondary school. As well as learning to speak English, they may also learn one of the three main languages too: Yoruba, Igbo or Hausa. By the age of 11, most children in Nigeria can already speak at least two languages. Although English is the official language of Nigeria, there are over 500 other languages spoken all over the country!

TRIBES

As the most populated country in the whole of Africa, there are over 250 different ethnic groups that live there, all with their own rich traditions, cultures and languages. There are three tribes in particular that account for just over half of the population of Nigeria: the Hausa, Yoruba and Igbo tribes.

The Hausa tribe make up around 30% of the population and originate in the Northwest part of Nigeria. Another indigenous group, located in Southwest Nigeria, are the Yoruba tribe. Renowned throughout history as talented sculptors, some of the Yoruba tribes are known to have created some of Africa's most famous artworks, like the Benin Bronzes from the 16th century.

The Igbo people (pronounced EE-BOH) make up around 18% of Nigeria's population and are known to have around 30 different dialects, which are all special and unique.

How many ethnic groups are in Nigeria?

EMPLOYMENT

Agriculture makes up most of Nigeria's work force with things like cocoa, yam and vegetables growing all around the country. Thanks to Nigeria and all the hardworking farmers that look after its land, approximately 8 million tons of rice is produced every year.

How much rice is produced every year?

FOOD

As well as yam and rice production, Nigeria is best known for its delicious, flavoursome food. Dishes like Jollof Rice and Pepper Soup are enjoyed by people all over the world!

NATURAL RESOURCES

Like many African countries, Nigeria has an abundance of natural resources. Natural gasses, oil and petroleum are things that are sent all over the world from Nigeria and are particularly important to the world economy.

INGREDIENTS

5 medium-sized tomatoes, roughly chopped
1 red bell pepper, roughly chopped
1 medium-sized onion, roughly chopped (set aside)
1/4 cup of oil
3 tbsp tomato paste
2 cups of parboiled rice
2 1/2 cups of chicken stock
1 tsp salt to taste
1/2 tsp curry powder
1/2 tsp thyme
1 tsp all-purpose seasoning
1 stock cube
3 bay leaves
water, as needed

JOLLOF RICE

Parboiling is the partial or semi boiling of food.

1. Blend the tomatoes and red pepper until smooth.

2. Using a medium-sized pot, fry the onions in the oil on a medium heat.

3. Once the onions are golden brown, add the tomato paste and fry for another 2-3 minutes.

4. Set aside ¼ of the blended tomatoes and add the rest. Fry for another 30 minutes. Keep stirring so that it doesn't burn.

5. Turn down the heat and add the chicken stock, seasoning, salt, curry powder, thyme and stock cube. Boil for another 10 minutes.

6. Add the parboiled rice and the bay leaves. Mix and add water until the rice is at the same level as the tomato mixture and chicken stock. Cover the pot and cook for another 15-30 minutes on a medium to low heat.

7. When the liquid has almost gone, add the rest of the blended tomatoes and cover. Cook for a further 5-10 minutes.

8. When the liquid has all dried up, turn off the heat. Your Jollof rice is ready to eat!

NIGERIA

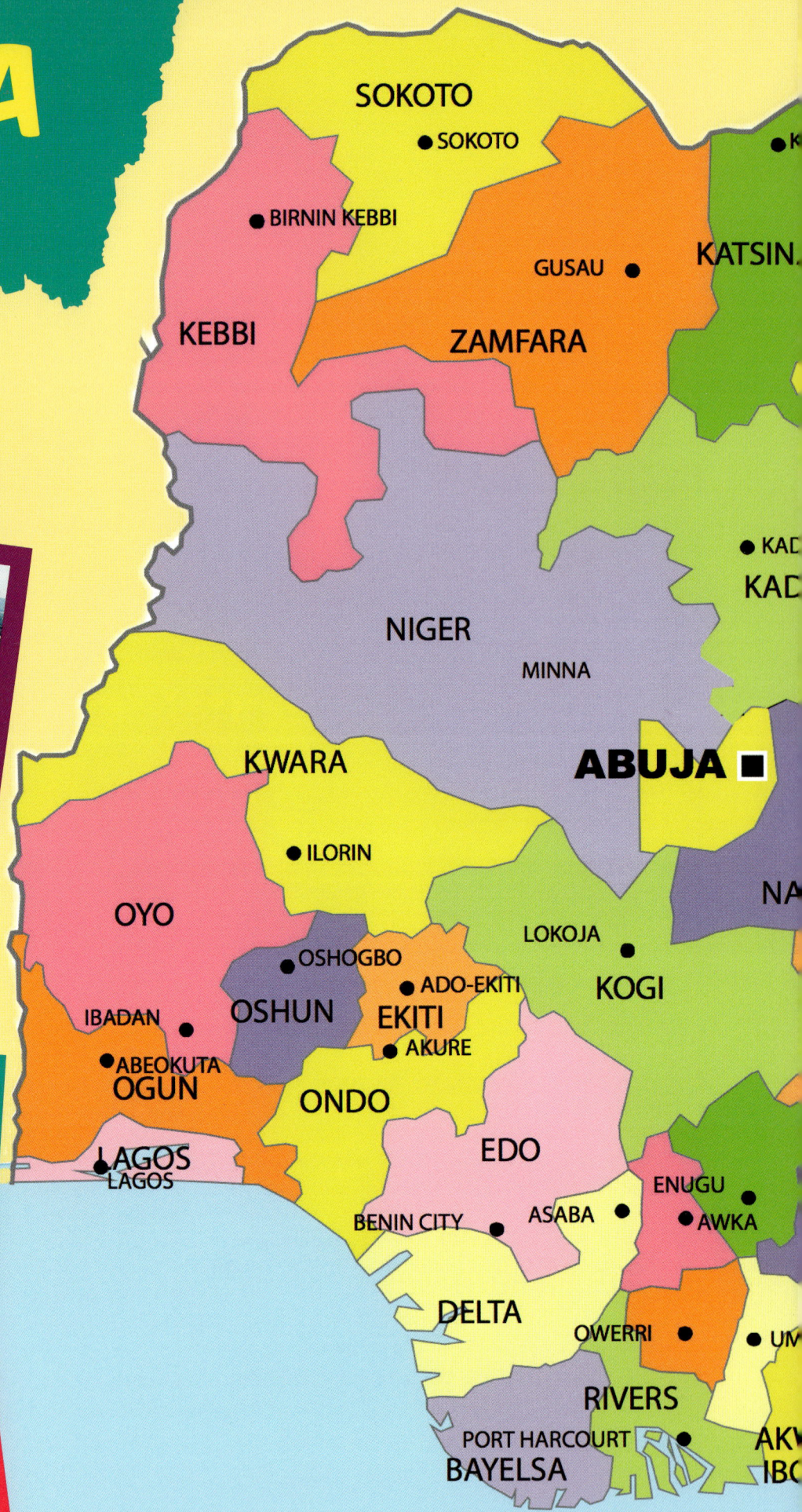

SOKOTO
- SOKOTO

BIRNIN KEBBI

KEBBI

GUSAU

KATSIN.

ZAMFARA

K

KAD

KAD

NIGER

MINNA

KWARA

ABUJA ◼

NA

ILORIN

OYO

OSHOGBO
LOKOJA

OSHUN

ADO-EKITI

KOGI

IBADAN

EKITI
AKURE

ABEOKUTA

OGUN

ONDO

LAGOS
LAGOS

EDO

ENUGU

BENIN CITY
ASABA
AWKA

DELTA

OWERRI
UM

RIVERS

PORT HARCOURT
AKW
IBO

BAYELSA

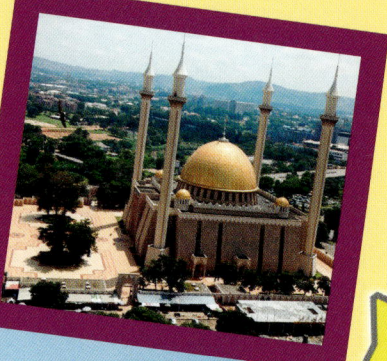

YOBE

JIGAWA

BORNO

DUTSE

KANO

ANO

DAMATURU

MAIDUGURI

BATA DRUM

BAUCHI

BAUCHI

GOMBE

GOMBE

JOS

A

ADAMAWA

YOLA

AYO

PLATEAU

JALINGO

LAFIA

RAWA

TARABA

URDI

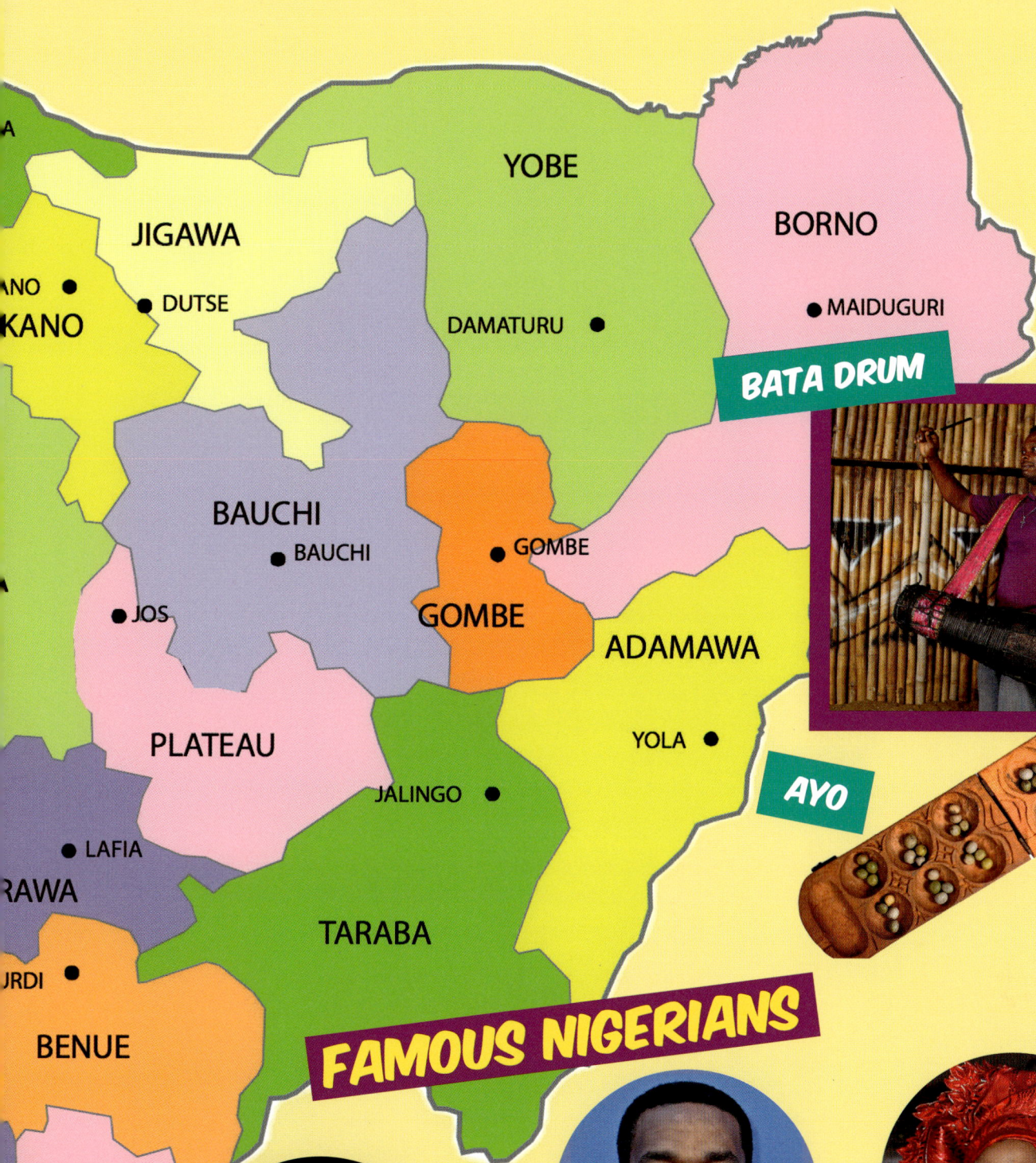

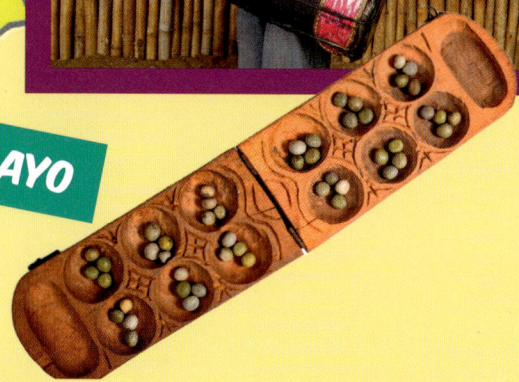

FAMOUS NIGERIANS

BENUE

CHIWETEL EJIOFOR

FOLORUNSHO ALAKIJA

BAKALIKI

ROSS
RIVER

FELA KUTI

CALABAR

GENEVIEVE NNAJI

ALIKO DANGOTE

Lewis Hamilton

You may have heard of Lewis Hamilton as the best Formula 1 driver in the world. He has won a total of seven championships and holds the world record for most F1 races won ... ever.

Lewis has also received a Knighthood for his impressive sportsmanship. A Knighthood means Lewis Hamilton can use the title 'Sir'. It is an award given by the Queen to people who achieve extraordinary things, like when Lewis won his first Formula 1 world championship for Britain in 2008.

As well as being a great race car driver, Lewis is also a serious fashion icon, musician and activist. He has spoken out on lots of issues, including the lack of diversity in his sport. Lewis set up 'The Hamilton Commission' to help encourage children, with positive role models, to get involved in subjects like mathematics, engineering, technology and science.

DID YOU KNOW?

Formula 1 is the biggest competition for race car drivers in the world. The fastest drivers all gather every year to compete in the F1 championships.

Lewis Hamilton is the only Black person to have ever raced in Formula 1.

LOANGO

KONGO

MATAMBA

NDONGO

ANGOLA

Nzinga had her soldiers trained in the skill of turning their bodies to attack and avoid blows through regular training. She also fought many battles at their side. She bragged, when she was nearly 80, that in her youth she was so agile and skilled in combat she could take on 25 armed men.

DID YOU KNOW?

WHO WAS ...
QUEEN NZINGA ?

1 Nzinga was born around 1583 in Ndongo, Southwest Africa.

2 As a child, Nzinga's father Ngola Mbandi Kiluanji, king of Ndongo, allowed her to enter battle at his side against other kingdoms and the Portuguese. He encouraged her to learn from the way he ruled his kingdom. Nzinga had an excellent education. She was well-spoken in her own language as well as Portuguese.

3 In 1622, Nzinga was sent to agree peace between the Ndongo and the Portuguese invaders on behalf of her brother, who was king at the time. She spoke in a strong and convincing way to the governor of Luanda and an agreement was made. The fighting stopped.

4 Around 1624, Nzinga became queen of Ndongo and queen of Matamba in 1630. The Portuguese did not recognise Nzinga as queen. They knew she would want her kingdoms to be independent and Nzinga would not want to be controlled by the Portuguese. Fighting began again and over the next 30 years Nzinga fought fiercely to protect her people from the Portuguese.

5 Nzinga is remembered as a great military leader. She used spies to collect useful information to plan attacks. Her soldiers joined the Portuguese army and then launched surprise attacks against them. The Dutch teamed up with Nzinga to defeat the Portuguese because they were impressed by her negotiation and organisation skills.

In 1657, realising that this was a fight they could not win, Portugal signed a treaty declaring that Ndongo was not under their control. Nzinga had been proving this for 30 years. Queen Nzinga died in 1663 at the age of around 80.

GRANDMA'S BANANA BREAD

Evett Joyce Billett-Allen was born in Trelawny, a parish in the county of Cornwall in Northwest Jamaica, on the 15th of September 1933. She loved to bake and here is one of her favourite banana bread recipes.

INGREDIENTS

2 cups of flour
1 tsp baking powder
1 pinch of salt
1 tsp ground nutmeg
1 tsp cinnamon
1/2 cup of soft butter
1 cup of brown sugar
2 beaten eggs
4-5 overripe bananas (mashed)
2 tsp vanilla extract
1/4 cup of raisins (optional)

LOVE

METHOD

Preheat oven to 175°C (350°F)

1. Sift the FLOUR and BAKING POWDER in a mixing bowl. Add NUTMEG, CINNAMON and SALT. Stir and set aside.
2. Mix the BUTTER and SUGAR together.
3. Add the EGGS and VANILLA to the mixture.
4. Add the mashed BANANAS and mix well.
5. Mix the dry ingredients with the wet ingredients and add RAISINS.
6. Pour the mixture into a greased loaf tin and bake at 175°C (350°F) for 60-65 MINUTES.
7. Once the banana bread has been taken out of the oven by an adult, let it cool down for ten minutes. Enjoy!

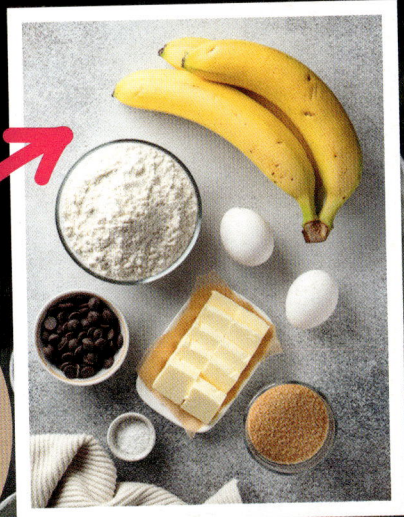

cocoa
loves

JOJO & GRAN GRAN

JoJo is a 4-year-old girl who loves spending time with her Gran Gran, while Mummy and Daddy are at work. She has a favourite toy called 'Panda' who goes everywhere with her. JoJo loves to play, especially if it involves dinosaurs! Her favourite book is about a pirate named 'Captain Chloe'. She also loves using Gran Gran's tablet to talk to her Great Gran Gran in St Lucia. Most importantly, JoJo loves Gran Gran and Gran Gran loves JoJo.

Gran Gran is JoJo's grandmother and always has something fun planned for when JoJo comes to visit. She is kind, playful and loves spending time with JoJo. Gran Gran is also very inventive and whenever there is a problem to solve, she always has a 'Gran Gran Plan' to save the day. Gran Gran lives on the same street as Jared, who runs the corner shop, and Cynthia, Gran Gran's neighbour who loves gardening and nature. Most importantly, Gran Gran loves JoJo and JoJo loves Gran Gran.

Watch JoJo & Gran Gran on CBeebies and BBC iPlayer.

JoJo & Gran Gran